Is Susan Here?

◆ by Janice May Udry ◆

◆ pictures by Karen Gundersheimer ◆

HarperCollins*Publishers*

Is Susan Here?
Text copyright © 1962, 1993 by Janice May Udry
Illustrations copyright © 1993 by Karen Gundersheimer
Printed in the U.S.A. All rights reserved.
1   2   3   4   5   6   7   8   9   10
New Edition

Library of Congress Cataloging-in-Publication Data
Udry, Janice May.
   Is Susan here? / by Janice May Udry ; illustrated by Karen
Gundersheimer. — New ed.
      p.   cm.
   Summary: When Susan disappears for the day, different animals
appear in her place and help Susan's mother and father with the
household chores.
   ISBN 0-06-026142-0. — ISBN 0-06-026143-9 (lib. bdg.)
   [1. Helpfulness—Fiction.   2. Parent and child—Fiction.]
I. Gundersheimer, Karen, ill.   II. Title.
PZ7.U27Is   1993   90-32044
[E]—dc20   CIP
                                                                 AC

One day right after breakfast, Susan disappeared.

But while Susan's mother was clearing the table, a something came into the kitchen.

"Mercy me!" said Susan's mother. "Whatever is this in my kitchen?"

"Grrr, it's a tiger," said the tiger. "Where is your little girl Susan?"

"I don't know," said Susan's mother. "But she usually helps me with the dishes."

"*I'll* help you today," said the tiger kindly.

So Susan's mother and the tiger did the dishes.

Then Susan's mother washed the clothes. Just as she started to hang them on the clothesline, an elephant came around the house.

It tugged at Susan's mother's apron with its trunk.

"Heavens!" said Susan's mother, dropping clothespins. "Where did you come from, Elephant?"

The elephant picked up the clothespins. "Where is your little girl Susan?" it asked.

"I don't know," said Susan's mother. "But she usually helps me hang up the clothes."

"*I'll* help you today," said the elephant kindly.

When Susan's father started to go to the market, a monkey met him at the door.

"Well," said Susan's father, "a monkey!"

On the way to the market, the monkey pushed the grocery cart and began to chatter.

"Where is your little girl Susan?" the monkey asked as they walked along.

"I don't know," said Susan's father. "But she usually goes to market with me."

"*I'll* go with you today," said the monkey. "I can do anything Susan can do."

Lunchtime came.

While Susan's father was stirring some soup, a pig came in.

"Oink," said the pig. "I'm hungry."

"Would you like to eat lunch with me?" asked Susan's father.

"Where is your little girl Susan?" asked the pig.

"I don't know," said Susan's father.

"Then *I* will eat lunch with you today," said the pig.

So Susan's father had lunch with a pig.

In the afternoon, Susan's mother said, "I'm going to take a little nap."

But as she was lying down on the couch, something walked up to her.

"Gracious! What is that?" asked Susan's mother.

"Grump, I'm a bear!"

"How do you do, Bear?" said Susan's mother rather sleepily.

"Grump," said the bear. "Don't you have a little girl Susan?"

"Yes, I do," said Susan's mother. "But she's not here. She usually takes a nap when I do."

The bear yawned. "I'll take Susan's nap today."

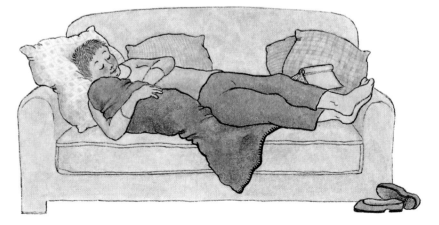

After her nap, Susan's mother began to sew.

A chicken came in and sat down next to her.

"Cluck, cluck. Is Susan here?" the chicken asked.

"No," said Susan's mother. "But she usually helps me with my sewing."

"Chickens are very good at pulling out stitches," said the chicken.

And the chicken pulled out the old hems on Susan's dresses so her mother could put in new ones.

Then Susan's father wrote a letter.

As he was stepping outside to mail it, a bird flew up to the door.

"My, what a large bird," said Susan's father.

"Twill-o, twill-o," sang the bird. "Is Susan here yet?"

"No," said Susan's father. "And she always mails my letters for me."

"*I'll* do it today," said the bird sweetly.

When dinner was ready, Susan's father and mother sat down to eat.

Before they had taken one bite, a rabbit joined them.

"My word," said Susan's father. "A rabbit!"

"Yes," said Susan's mother. "This house is full of animals."

"Is your little girl Susan coming to dinner?" asked the rabbit.

"No, I guess not," said Susan's mother.

"Then I'll eat Susan's dinner," said the rabbit, picking up a fork. "Pass the carrots, please."

"For a rabbit," said Susan's father, "you certainly do eat a lot."

After dinner, Susan's mother and father sat down in their big, comfortable chairs. It was very quiet.

"I miss Susan," sighed Susan's mother.

"I miss Susan too," said Susan's father.

"It was nice to be helped today by a tiger, an elephant, a monkey, a pig, a bear, a chicken, and a bird, and to have dinner with a rabbit," said Susan's mother. "But I'd rather have dear Susan."

"Do you suppose she will ever come back?" asked Susan's father.

"Who knows?" sighed Susan's mother. "And we have no one to put to bed tonight. I think I'll just go sit awhile in Susan's room, even though she is not there."

"I think I'll go sit awhile in Susan's room with you," said Susan's father. "Even though she is not there."

So they went into Susan's room.

Susan's mother sat down in the rocking chair. She even sang the song Susan liked best to hear at night.

Then, very softly, someone came in.
"I'm back," said Susan.

And she was.